JUNGLE 2 JUNGLE

ADAPTED BY
Nancy Krulik

A Junior Novel by Nancy Krulik
Based on *"Un Indien Dans La Ville"* written
by Hervè Palud, Thierry Lhermitte,
Igor Aptekman and Philippe Bruneau de la Salle
Screenplay by Bruce A. Evans & Raynold Gideon

DISNEY
PRESS

New York

SPECIAL EDITION

Printed in the United States of America.

This book is set in 11-point Leawood Book.

Library of Congress Catalog Card Number: 96-71631

ISBN:0-7868-4193-1

CHAPTER ONE

"COME FORWARD."

The chief's bellowing voice shook Mimi Siku to the core. But the boy did not show his fear. He had waited all twelve years of his life for this manhood ceremony. Now, here he was, standing on a cliff with the other boys his age, his face painted red, his heart filled with pride. Mimi Siku was ready to take his place as an adult in the Pinare Tribe.

Mimi Siku stepped up and watched as the Pinare chief raised a rolled-up banana leaf to his lips. With a strong breath, the chief blew a shower of green powdery flakes onto Mimi Siku's face, shoulders, and chest. Mimi Siku rubbed the powder from his bright brown eyes and took a deep breath.

The ancient test of manhood had begun!

With nerves of steel, Mimi Siku took a deep breath and dove headfirst off the cliff. He flew through the air, faster and faster, until finally he landed with a splash in the cool clear waters of the tropical river.

Mimi Siku climbed up on the riverbank. Cautiously, he made his way through the thick

Venezuelan rain forest, searching for his prey. He finally spied a fat, lazy lizard sunning itself on a rock. Silently, the boy raised his bow and arrow—and . . . *THUNK!* The reptile was skewered. Mimi Siku grinned. It would make a tasty dinner.

The boy tied the lizard to his brown leather loincloth. He reached into a small pouch and pulled out a handful of a thick, sticky substance. Then he climbed straight up a huge rock cliff. The sticky stuff helped his hands cling to the rock.

That evening, Mimi Siku cooked the lizard over a campfire. As the last sliver of the sun set in the sky, the boy let out a loud, joyous shout. He had learned his lessons well.

Mimi Siku had finally become a man!

CHAPTER TWO

Three thousand miles away, forty-one-year-old Michael Cromelin was going through his own test of manhood—on the floor of the New York Coffee, Sugar, and Cocoa Exchange. It took nerves of steel to stand his ground in the pit of the exchange. Thousands of traders were bidding for the same items, and only the wisest of traders knew when to bid and when to hold.

"Do I hear ninety-five and a quarter?" the coffee broker called out into the crowd.

Michael shook his head. That price was too high. "Ninety-four and three-quarters," he countered.

The broker looked around for a better offer. None came. The broker sighed. Ninety-four and three-quarters! "Sold!" he said.

Yes! Michael congratulated himself. He felt he'd made a great deal. Unfortunately, his partner, Richard Kempster, didn't agree.

"Michael, what was that?" Richard asked frantically, as he fidgeted with the lapel of his green trader's jacket. Richard had a tendency to fidget when he was nervous—which was just about all the time. "Three hundred lots of coffee futures? You call that a hunch?"

Michael calmly shook his head. "I call it an opportunity," he replied confidently.

"Three hundred lots in this market isn't an opportunity," Richard insisted. "It's a death wish!"

"O ye of little faith," Michael said.

"No, me of big mortgage," Richard muttered as he followed Michael off the trading floor and into the lobby of the exchange.

Madeleine, Michael's earnest, trustworthy secretary, was waiting for them. She handed Michael his passport and an airplane ticket.

"It's American flight 109, leaving JFK at 1 P.M. and arriving in Caracas at 6:22 P.M.," she told Michael.

Richard looked incredulously at his partner. "You're not still going—not after what you did in there!" he demanded.

Michael shook his head. Richard could be such a worrywart. "I'm marrying Charlotte in a month," he explained to Richard, "and to do that, I have to divorce Patricia. And to do *that,* I have to go to Caracas!"

Richard watched as Madeleine handed Michael his suitcase and his laptop computer.

"You're leaving me with 5,100 tons of coffee in my lap!" he cried.

Michael put the plane ticket in his jacket pocket

and headed out into the street. "Richard, the only reason I've put up with you for so long is because you are the best analyst around. And that's because you're never motivated by money. You live for the trade."

Michael rested a calm hand on Richard's twitching shoulder. "Trust me," he said. "We'll get ninety-seven and a half."

Richard shook his head. "You give me that same speech whenever you play one of your stupid hunches."

"And what happens?" Michael asked with a self-assured grin.

As he covered himself with a thin airline blanket, Michael looked out at the clouds below. He sighed contentedly. At this time tomorrow, he would be a free man. Michael had a hunch things were going to go very smoothly in Caracas.

Michael didn't know it, but for once, his hunch was wrong!

CHAPTER THREE

The plane touched down on the runway at sunset. Michael stepped out into the hot Caracas evening. It was hard to believe, but it was even hotter here than it had been in New York.

Michael searched the airport for his ride. Finally he saw a huge, dark-haired man holding a teeny-tiny sign. The sign said MICHAEL KROMELIN.

Michael walked over and handed the man his suitcase. "I'm Michael Cromelin," he said. "That's Cromelin with a C."

"Señor Cromelin with a C, I am Abe Botero, your attorney-at-law," the man greeted Michael in a thick Spanish accent. "I am outrageously pleased to meet with you. I have an automobile right this way and might I inquire if you are in possession of any other luggage?"

Michael rolled his eyes. "Am I paying you by the word?" he asked with disgust.

Abe Botero laughed, which annoyed Michael even further. "This is all I have," Michael declared. "Look, I know it's late, but is there any possibility of meeting with Patricia tonight?"

Abe shook his head and held up a small white envelope. "We received a letter today . . ." he began.

Michael grabbed the envelope from his hands and tore it open. His eyes quickly scanned the page. He couldn't understand a word.

"It's in Spanish," he said.

"Señora Cromelin was unable to make it to Caracas," Abe translated. "She asked that we come to Moura."

Michael's face turned beet red. "Moura?" he shouted. "Whoa! Wait a second! I fly 3,000 miles to meet her here and she doesn't show up? Okay. If this is the way she's going to play, she's not going to get a dime! Where the hell is Moura?"

Abe turned to a laminated map of South America that was tacked to the wall behind them. He pointed at a tiny dot. "Here," he said simply.

"That's in the middle of nowhere!" Michael exclaimed. Then he sighed. It was obvious that Patricia was up to something. But what? There was only one way to find out.

Before he knew it, Michael found himself on a small, ramshackle, two-engine plane headed for Moura.

The trip to Moura seemed endless to Michael. When they finally touched down at the tiny makeshift airport, it was almost dawn. The rain was pouring, and the wind was thrashing through the trees. But Michael Cromelin was on a mission. Nothing could stop him. He grabbed a huge, thick banana leaf, and using it as an umbrella, made his way to number 27.

"Here it is, 27," Michael told Abe. "She lives there?"

The lawyer pointed to the red and white sign above their heads.

"It is the postal office. She must be the postman," Abe suggested.

Michael shrugged. He had no idea what Patricia had been doing since she left him almost thirteen years ago. Postman was as good a guess as any.

But it wasn't Patricia who answered Michael's knock at the door. It was a very sleepy, very angry man.

"Hi," Michael greeted him. "Is Patricia Cromelin here?"

The postman stared blankly at Michael. Then he turned to Abe and said something in Spanish. The two men spoke back and forth for quite a while before bursting into laughter.

"You're going to laugh very largely at this," Abe said to Michael. "Señora Cromelin is not here."

Michael wasn't laughing.

"She left you a letter," Abe said, handing another small white envelope to his client.

Michael tore the letter from his hand. His eyes

bulged when he read the note. Patricia wanted to meet him in some place called Lipo Lipo.

Obviously this divorce was going to take longer than he'd thought. He knew he had to check in with Richard. He asked to borrow the postman's phone and quickly dialed the office.

"I'm standing in the middle of *Nightmare on Bodega Street*," Michael complained. "But I'll get back as fast as I can."

"If you don't get back, do I sell or do I hold?" Richard asked nervously.

"Do not sell until I give you the say-so. Call me on the uplink when London opens," Michael said. Then he hung up and turned to Abe. "What's the fastest way to Lipo Lipo?" he asked.

"You can get there," Abe said, with his typical laugh. He pointed to a tiny dot on the post office map. "But not from here."

Michael nodded. He would get to Lipo Lipo all right. But he wasn't taking that laughing hyena of a lawyer with him! Quickly he raced down to the river-bank and hailed the first dugout canoe he could find.

Lipo Lipo, here I come, he thought.

CHAPTER FOUR

The boatman gunned the outboard motor and sped down the river. Michael took out his handkerchief and dipped it into the cool water.

"I wouldn't do that," the boatman warned.

"Why not?" Michael asked.

"Piranha, that's why," the boatman explained.

Quickly, Michael yanked up his hand. Six blue-gray, flesh-eating piranhas dangled ominously from the handkerchief. One bit into Michael's hand with razor sharp teeth. "AAAAHHHHH!" he screamed out in pain.

As Michael bandaged his injured fingers, the boat-man rounded a bend and eased the canoe to a stop by a small native village.

"Lipo Lipo," he said, pointing to the huts.

Michael stepped gingerly out of the boat. "I'll be right back," he told the boatman as stepped ashore.

"Not long," the boatman warned. "I have an appointment."

Michael looked around. There was nothing but huts, water, and jungle. "You have an appointment?"

he exclaimed in disbelief. "If it's the cable guy, you've got plenty of time, believe me!"

A group of natives surrounded Michael. "Hi. Peace," Michael said, raising his hand like a character in an old Western. "I'm looking for Patricia Cromelin."

The Pinare tribe members stared at him. They didn't understand a word he said.

"She looks like me," Michael said, indicating his pale skin and light eyes. "She's a doctor. A woman." Michael moved his hands in an hourglass shape to demonstrate a woman's body.

The Pinare caught on. "Paliku," one of them said. The others nodded and turned toward the village. Michael followed close behind.

The group led Michael to the largest hut in the village. He walked in and saw a big woman's butt staring back at him.

"Patricia?" he asked nervously, looking at the cloth-covered rump.

A bamboo screen moved off to the side. A small, thin woman with dark hair and soft brown eyes appeared from behind it.

"Michael! You made it!" Patricia said.

"Despite your best efforts," Michael grumbled.

Patricia sighed. "Defensive as ever," she said. "You look good. How have you been?"

Michael stared at her. How had he been? He'd been up for more than twenty-four hours, caught in a torrential rainstorm, bitten by piranhas . . . "Never been better," he replied sarcastically. Patricia hunched down next to the large woman Michael had seen when he'd entered the hut.

"Botako's having her first litter," she said.

"Congratulations," Michael told the woman.

Patricia laughed. "Not her. This is Pontspie." Patricia turned to the woman and said, "This is Michael," in a language Michael had never heard before.

"Hi, Pontspie," Michael said. Pontspie smiled flirtatiously. Michael gulped.

Patricia pointed to a weak pig that was in labor. "This is Botako, Pontspie's sow." The pig let out a piercing cry of pain.

Michael shook the noise from his ears. "Patricia, I hate to spoil this joyous event, but I've come all the way from New York, and I have a boat waiting. Is there some place we can talk in private?"

"Paliku," Patricia replied. "My Pinare name is Paliku. It means armpit without hair."

Michael stared at his soon-to-be-ex-wife. "There's really no comeback to a line like that, is there?" he asked. "Okay, *Paliku*," he continued, "you remember one day thirteen years ago, totally out of the blue, after we'd been married all of a year, when you walked out on me and disappeared?"

"I remember. And now you want a divorce. So

who's the lucky girl?" Patricia asked. She knew that the only reason Michael would leave his work to get a divorce was to marry someone else.

"She's no one you know," Michael replied. "And considering the facts, I don't think it would be fair for you to ask for a large settlement."

Patricia looked Michael straight in the eye. "I don't want any money."

Now Michael was *really* surprised. After all, "I don't want any money" were not words Wall Street traders heard every day.

"So if you don't want any money, why did you drag me all the way here?"

Patricia didn't answer. She was busy delivering a piglet.

"It's a boy," she announced, holding up the tiny squealing animal.

"The family name lives on," Michael mumbled with disgust. "Look. My canoe is waiting. If we leave right now, we can go to Caracas, sign the papers, and I can be back in New York by tomorrow."

Patricia shook her head. "I can't leave," she said, plopping two wet, squealing pigs in Michael's arms. "Tomorrow is the Fantenyou celebration and I have to be here."

"But I have to get moving," Michael insisted. "My boatman has an appointment and I . . ."

Michael was interrupted by two young Pinare children. They ran up to the doorway and shouted something at Patricia.

"Your boatman is gone," Patricia translated.

"What?!" Michael cried out. He raced to the beach and shouted after the retreating boatman. "What you are doing is highly unprofessional!"

Behind Michael, a group of children had already gathered. They were unpacking his things. And they were fascinated by them. One of the boys had Michael's boxer shorts pulled over his head—he was scaring the other kids by pretending to be a monster! Another child was painting his face with Michael's toothpaste.

Michael looked at the scene in horror. How had he gotten himself into this mess? Here he was, stuck on some bizarre island with his ex-wife, a group of squealing piglets, and a gang of kids who thought his underwear was the most fascinating thing they'd ever seen.

Patricia laughed at his predicament. "You can spend the night with the bachelors," she suggested. "Or Pontspie offered to share her hut."

The heavyset woman winked at Michael and waved. Michael smiled nervously. He'd take his chances with the bachelors.

CHAPTER FIVE

That evening, Michael sat beside Patricia on a drift-wood stump. Cooking fires burned around them.

"Hungry?" Patricia asked as she handed him a platter of small meat patties.

"Starving," Michael replied. He looked curiously at the meat.

"It's yellow-eared bat. A local specialty. It's made from the bladder."

Michael's stomach turned over. "Bat bladder," he grimaced. "Holy Kaopectate! No, thanks!"

Patricia gently took the plate from Michael's hands and handed it to a member of the Pinare tribe. She took a deep breath and looked Michael in the eye.

"There's something I have to talk to you about, Michael," she said quietly. "Something you don't know."

Michael glanced at her big brown eyes and kicked at the ground. "Is this where you tell me why you left me?"

"I left you because of the fifth phone line," Patricia said simply.

"The what?"

"One morning a man showed up at the apartment to install a fifth phone line," Patricia continued. "He asked me if I was the receptionist. Suddenly I realized—I was. So I packed my things and left."

Michael shook his head in disbelief. "No explanation. No idea where you were going. My wife is gone and all I'm left with is a note that says you're leaving and not to follow you."

"It was the only way I could go on loving you," Patricia explained.

Michael's eyes opened wide. "You sure have a funny way of showing it," he barked. "I couldn't sleep for two years. I was the only one awake in the New York office when the Singapore market opened. I guess I have you to thank for making me the expert on Asian markets," he said sarcastically.

Patricia nodded calmly. "It's hard for me to tell you this, and you have every right to be angry, but *please* listen."

Michael leaned back and folded his arms. "What else can I do?" he demanded. "I'm stuck here with you and the village people until after the Fantenyou."

Ding! Their conversation was interrupted by a loud alarm. A message was coming through on Michael's laptop.

"Excuse me," Michael said. "The real world is calling." He raced over and sat in front of his computer. The Pinare chief and some of the other village elders watched with fascination as Michael typed a message. Within seconds, a reply flashed on the screen. Coffee was selling for ninety-seven and a quarter. Michael raised his hands in victory. Once again, he was right.

Patricia watched as Michael stared at the numbers flashing across the screen. Same old Michael. Work always came first.

"Michael, what I'm trying to tell you is hard to say but—but I wasn't alone when I left you."

Michael nodded as though he were listening. But Patricia knew better. Still, she kept talking.

"I didn't know it, but I was pregnant," she declared. "I left with your child. Your son."

It was earth-shattering news. But Michael didn't react. He was too busy waiting for coffee to reach ninety-seven and a half. And it did. Michael tapped a key, and the deal was set. "Sold for a tidy profit of $300,000 in one day! It's good to be good!" he said.

Michael turned to Patricia. "What were you saying?" he asked.

But Patricia was already gone. As far as she was concerned, things hadn't changed a bit in thirteen years. Michael stood and took off after her so quickly he didn't even notice that a new message had appeared on his screen. CONFIRM TRANSMISSION, the message said.

* * *

Michael found Patricia sitting quietly by the beach. He sat down and looked curiously at her. "What's the matter?" he asked. "What did I do?"

Patricia sighed angrily. "I just told you we had a son, and you didn't even hear me."

Michael's eyes bulged from his head. "A son!" he croaked nervously. "What son? What are you talking about? A son?"

"Your son." Patricia pointed to a boy sitting by the fire. "That boy is your son."

Michael stared at the young man. He looked about twelve. He was dressed like the other children, and his skin was tanned by the sun, but it was obvious that he was not a native Pinare. The boy looked at Michael, and for the first time their eyes met.

"At first I was angry," Patricia confessed. "Then I was scared. I must have started at least a thousand letters to you."

Michael stood and stared angrily at Patricia. "This is unforgivable!" he declared.

Patricia nodded. "I'm not asking you to forgive me," she said. "But it's not his fault. He didn't do anything. Blame me. Not him."

Michael sat silent until the truth could sink in. Finally he said slowly, "That's my son."

"His name is Mimi Siku."

"Mimi Siku," Michael repeated, letting the sound of the words roll off his tongue.

"Roughly translated, it means 'cat piss,' " Patricia explained. "Kids here choose their own names on their eighth birthday."

"Darn. And I was so hoping to call my first son 'dog poop.' It's a family tradition, you know," Michael rambled, "and then there's the monograms on the silverware and everything else. . . ."

Patricia shook her head. "Typical Michael," she said. "In the face of emotion, revert to sarcasm."

Now Michael was really angry. How *dare* Patricia try to tell him how to react. "You just finished telling me you stole my kid from me twelve years ago and waited until now to tell me. If sarcasm's the worst you get from me, you're lucky!" he shouted.

Michael was about to continue when he heard strange noises coming from his computer. He raced back to discover the entire village playing with the keyboard. Then suddenly a huge warning flashed across the screen:

RECHARGE BATTERIES. RECHARGE BATTERIES.

Michael watched in horror as the screen went black.

That night, Michael tried to sleep pretzeled in a hammock. He couldn't believe his bad luck. Here he was, stuck without a computer in a place that made *Gilligan's Island* look like Club Med.

19

CHAPTER SIX

Sometime in the middle of the night Michael made a wrong turn in his hammock. He landed facedown with a *thud* on the ground. As he struggled to his feet, he came face to face with a set of eyes that looked remarkably like his own.

"Mimi Siku?" Michael asked.

Mimi smiled.

"Hi. I'm Michael Cromelin," he said. "Patricia, I mean Paliku, tells me I'm your father. Your old man. Pops." Michael held out his hand.

The boy stared at him curiously, then reached out and shook his father's hand.

Michael's eyes drifted down to a small copper pot Mimi held in his left hand.

"Nice pot," Michael said.

Mimi answered him—in Pinare.

"Do you speak English?" Michael asked the boy.

Again Mimi replied in Pinare.

This was going to be tougher than Michael had thought. "Well, your mother wants me to say something, you know, fatherly," Michael began. The boy stared at him blankly. But Michael talked on. "Okay, I'm not very good at this. But I don't regret anything. Well, maybe I have a few regrets. But then again, too few to mention.

"'You know, there were times, I'm sure you knew, that I bit off more than I could chew,'" Michael continued, borrowing the lyrics from an old Frank Sinatra song. "'But through it all, when there was doubt, I ate it up and spit it out. I faced it all, and I stood tall, and did it my way.'"

Mimi stared at Michael. Then he turned and walked outside.

Michael watched as Mimi made his way over to a girl and handed her his copper pot. The two giggled and walked away.

"Well, it worked for me," Michael muttered, as he struggled back into his hammock.

The next morning, Michael awoke with a start. Patricia was shouting, "Michael, Michael!" in his ear.

Michael opened one eye just a slit and glanced around.

"Mimi Siku wants you," Patricia explained.

"Oh right, my son," Michael replied, wiping the sleep from his eyes. "I was just dreaming this was all a dream."

"No dream," Patricia assured him. "Come on. He's waiting."

Michael tried carefully to get out of the hammock, but somehow he managed to land facedown on the ground with a thud again.

"These things should come with air bags," Michael complained. Then he turned to Patricia. "Last night I told him I was his father. I don't know if he understood, though. All he did was say something in Pinare and give some girl a pot."

"Giving a pot here is like giving flowers," Patricia explained. "It's a love gift. Mimi is very popular with the girls."

Michael's chest swelled with pride. "I guess he *is* mine," he grinned.

Patricia laughed. "He's yours. And he wants to take you to lunch."

"Great," Michael agreed. "Italian? Chinese?"

Patricia smiled. "Just go," she prodded him.

Michael stood up and tried to smile. Lunch. On some strange island where they thought bat bladder was a delicacy, with a son he'd never met before. This had to be some sort of hoax. A joke. Michael peered around the hut. He was looking for a hidden camera.

There wasn't any.

CHAPTER SEVEN

Michael walked down to the beach, where Mimi Siku was waiting beside a canoe. Obviously, they would have to travel to their luncheon spot.

As father and son paddled along the river, they tried to communicate. They passed a family of monkeys playing on some rocks.

"*Baboon. Baboon*," Mimi Siku said.

"Monkeys," Michael said, offering the English translation.

Mimi Siku nodded and cupped his hands through the clear water. "*Toona, toona*," he said in Pinare.

"Water," Michael said in English. He drifted his hands through the cold liquid and screamed. A vicious fish was clamped to his pointer finger. "Piranha!" he shouted.

Mimi Siku giggled. Then the sound of a bird caught his attention. "*Hoko*," he told his father.

Michael nodded. "Hoko. Bird. Bird who can't sing, Hoko Ono," he joked.

Mimi shook his head. "No," he declared. "Toucan is hoko. Bird is *pomoko*."

Michael was shocked. "Wait a minute!" he exclaimed. "You speak English?"

Mimi nodded. "Paliku teach me. 'Mary can a little ham, its fleas were right as snow.' This story Stephen King," the boy recited proudly.

Michael blushed. That meant the kid understood all those ridiculous things he'd said the night before—about doing it his way. "Oh, no!" Michael moaned.

But Mimi Siku didn't seem to think Michael was silly. He actually seemed kind of proud. "Paliku tell me you big trader in your village. Me should be proud of you," the boy said. "Now you see. Me good trader, too," he boasted as he pulled the canoe alongside a boat full of pots, bows, and arrows. Mimi Siku handed the trader a small golden stone. In exchange, the trader handed Mimi a small pot.

"Wait a second," Michael warned, pulling his son aside.

"What problem?" Mimi asked impatiently.

"You're gonna give him a nugget of gold for that?" Michael asked, pointing to the small pot. "I hate to tell you, but he's robbing you blind, kid."

Mimi Siku tried not to smile. "That not gold," he explained. "Just a pretty stone."

Once again, Michael blushed. "Oh, in that case, great. Deal's fine," he told the trader.

Michael was ready to head back to the village. But Mimi still had much he wanted to share with his new-found father. Before long, Michael found himself wandering through the underbrush of the jungle. As he followed his son around a bush, Michael heard a soft hissing sound. Suddenly, he came face-to-face with a huge snake! The snake eyed Michael carefully then reared up to strike. In one short second the snake bared its fangs, hissed, and . . . toppled to the ground.

Mimi Siku had shot the snake with a blowgun dart and saved his father's life!

The boy bent down, picked up the snake, and offered it to his father. Michael moved far away.

"Scared?" Mimi Siku asked.

Michael nervously shook his head. "Are you kidding me?" he asked. "Some of my best friends are snakes." He reached over and tentatively took the long, dry-skinned creature from Mimi. Then he confidently wrapped the snake around his waist like an exotic leather belt.

"This would go great with my gray Armani suit," he laughed. "Is this a dangerous snake?"

Mimi nodded. "*Buradu* bite make body swell, neck turn black, blood leak from nose," he explained.

Suddenly Michael felt the snake's head twitch. He jumped up in fright. "You sure this thing's dead?" he asked.

"Not dead, sleeping," Mimi said calmly, as he took the snake from his father's waist. *Crunch.* The boy bit through the snake's spine. "Now dead," he said simply, as he draped the snake around his neck and walked away.

Finally it was lunchtime. Michael and Mimi Siku sat alone at a campfire, eating the snake. Michael was surprised to discover it wasn't all that bad. A little like chicken.

Mimi Siku took Michael's hand and slapped a wad of wet meat into his palm. "Monkey guts," the boy explained. "Taste good."

Michael gulped and put the wad of flesh back into his son's hand. "No. No," he insisted. He patted his stomach dramatically. "Snake fill me up good."

Mimi shrugged and wolfed down the food. Then he looked at Michael and asked nervously, "Now you here, you stay with me all the time?"

Michael shifted in his seat. "I'd really like that Mimi Siku, but I can't," he answered, as gently as possible.

"If you stay, me teach you to fish, to hunt, to plant yucca."

Michael looked away. "Tomorrow me must go home. Make many big trades," he said.

Mimi nodded sadly. Then he held out a small silver charm that he wore on a rope around his neck. Michael looked at the charm curiously. It was a tiny Statue of Liberty.

"This is in your village, yes?" Mimi asked. "Woman who hold fire up sky's behind?"

"The Statue of Liberty?" Michael replied, choking

back a laugh. "I've never quite heard her described as that, but yes, the Statue of Liberty is in my village."

Mimi seemed pleased. "You take me there?" he asked.

Michael shrugged. "Sure, someday," he replied.

"When me man, you take me to the Statue of Liberty?" Mimi continued.

Michael looked at the twelve-year-old. Sure, in six or seven years he could take the kid to the Statue of Liberty. That was a commitment he could handle. "You've got yourself a deal," he assured him.

Mimi held up his hand for a high five. "*Wakatepe*," he said.

Michael slapped the boy's hand. "Wakatepe."

It was a deal. But for once, Michael Cromelin didn't know what kind of deal he was getting into!

Michael watched as Mimi Siku struggled to keep his eyes open. Michael chuckled to himself. The kid still took afternoon naps, he thought. Of course, an afternoon of killing poisonous snakes and eating monkey guts could do that to a person.

Before long, the boy settled into a quiet sleep. Michael got up, sauntered over toward the river, and threw out the rest of the monkey guts. Then he went back to check on Mimi Siku, and . . . *screamed*! There was a gigantic tarantula crawling across the boy's chest!

"Mimi, don't move!" Michael cried out. "There's a huge spider on you!"

Mimi's eyes fluttered open. The threatened spider scurried off Mimi's arm and charged across the sand at Michael.

Michael raced down toward the water. The spider followed close behind.

"Get away from me!" Michael screamed at the angry arachnid. He picked up a rock and tried to bean the spider, but he missed. The spider kept coming. Michael leaped onto a log in the water.

"Stop! Stop!" Michael cried out. "I don't want to hurt you! Get back! I swear I'll crush you like a bug!" *Splash!* Michael lost his balance and fell into the water.

Mimi sat up and started to laugh. He walked over and gently picked up the spider.

"You scream, Maitika attack. You calm, Maitika nice," Mimi explained, holding the spider up to his father. But *kukuve* always mean," Mimi continued.

"Who's Kukuve?" Michael asked, as he caught his breath.

Mimi pointed to a crocodile sneaking up behind his father. Michael turned slowly, took one look at the creature's sharp teeth, and shot like a rocket out of the water.

"THIS PLACE IS A NIGHTMARE!" Michael screeched, as he ran toward the shore.

CHAPTER EIGHT

As night fell, Michael found himself taking part in a sacred Pinare ceremony, dressed in nothing but a loincloth and palm headdress. It was definitely *not* Armani!

The drumbeat grew quicker and quicker. Children raced past Michael and shouted "Baboon. Baboon." Michael wasn't quite sure what that meant, but somehow he figured it wasn't a compliment.

"The hair on your chest reminds them of monkeys," Patricia whispered. "Baboon is your Pinare name."

Michael was about to make a remark when Mimi Siku and another boy were suddenly pulled out of the dance by the chief. The chief stood before them and pounded at the earth with a long, thick stick and chanted loudly.

"He's telling the forest that these two boys are no longer children," Patricia explained.

Suddenly the witch doctor, in a blonde wig and black grass skirt, emerged from the circle of dancers. He pulled a smoldering branch from the fire and carried it over to the chief, who accepted the branch and held it out to the boy standing beside Mimi. The boy grabbed the glowing tip of the branch and held on until the chief motioned for him to let go.

Now it was Mimi Siku's turn. The boy wrapped his hand around the hottest spot. Michael winced, but Mimi Siku's face showed no sign of pain.

Finally Mimi let go of the stick. "Is he finished?" Michael asked hopefully.

Patricia shook her head. "Almost. But in order to be a tribal leader someday, he has to perform a task that the chief chooses for him."

The chief approached Patricia and Michael and began to speak in a loud, deep voice.

"He's saying he's proud of Mimi Siku, and as his father, you should be, too," Patricia translated.

"I'm proud as I can be," Michael replied.

The chief turned and stood above Mimi Siku. It was time for him to receive his task.

"He's given Mimi Siku the task of bringing fire back from the Statue of Liberty," Patricia whispered in Michael's ear.

"You promised to take me to New York when I became a man," Mimi Siku reminded his father.

"And when you are a man, I will," Michael smiled.

Patricia smirked. "He's a man *now*, and he wants to go," she said. "The chief gave him this task because you told him you'd take him to New York."

30

"Maybe I did," Michael stuttered. He turned to Mimi. "But I have to be back on the exchange floor. I'm about to get married. Can't do tomorrow."

Now Patricia was angry. Really angry! "The exchange floor! Tomorrow! Maybe! Those words don't exist here!" she shouted.

"That's not my fault!" Michael responded. "You're the one who came to live with the Pirates of the Caribbean! And you're his mother. He should speak better English. And by the way, Stephen King did not write *Mary Had a Little Ham*!"

"You're going to humiliate him in front of his whole tribe?" Patricia asked in disbelief.

"Looks that way, doesn't it?" Michael snapped back.

"You make wakatepe with me, Baboon," Mimi said, as he turned and walked away.

Michael watched the boy leave. He felt really bad letting him down. Michael sighed. This kid was good. *Really good.*

But why not—Mimi *was* his kid, after all.

And so, the next morning, Michael found himself paying for a second ticket to New York City.

There were just two tiny problems. How was he going to handle a kid who walked around in a loincloth and ate monkey guts? And worse yet, how was he going to explain him to Charlotte?!

CHAPTER NINE

Richard shifted back and forth as he waited at the airport terminal for Michael. Finally, Richard saw Michael. He was so relieved to see his partner, he didn't even notice the suntanned twelve-year-old dressed in a loincloth and headband riding the escalator behind him.

"Michael! Michael!" Richard called out. He leaped onto the escalator and raced up in the wrong direction until he reached him.

"Richard, what are you doing here?" Michael asked with surprise.

"I told Latshaw you had a reason. You *do* have a reason, don't you?" Richard asked nervously.

Michael stared at Richard. What was he talking about? Michael had the odd feeling that he had stepped in the middle of a conversation that had already started. He looked around. There was nobody there. Richard was definitely talking to him. "A reason for what?" Michael asked finally.

"A reason for holding onto the beans," Richard said.

Michael stared at Richard. "You didn't sell them?" he asked.

"No."

Michael could not believe his ears. "I told you to sell them at ninety-seven and a half!" he declared.

Richard nearly doubled over with nerves. "Oh my God!" he cried. "I'm dead! I'm going to lose my house! I moved away to the country to reduce stress, and look, my pulse is up to 180!" He held out his wrist to Michael.

"Why didn't you sell?" Michael asked.

Richard looked at him incredulously. "You didn't confirm! That's why!" he said.

Somehow, Michael managed to remain calm. "Where's coffee now?" he asked.

"It's under ninety cents and limit down," Richard sighed.

"I said to sell at ninety-seven and a half," Michael insisted again.

"But you didn't confirm. For fifteen years now, you say, 'sell,' and I say, 'confirm.' Then you say, 'sell,' and I sell. Sell, confirm. Sell, confirm. Sell, confirm," Richard repeated over and over. "You didn't confirm."

Suddenly the twelve-year-old in the loincloth and headband made his way over to Michael and Richard.

"Get out of here," Richard told the boy. "I already gave at the rain forest."

Michael sighed. *Mimi Siku.* In all the confusion, he'd practically forgotten the kid.

"He's my son," Michael explained simply.

Richard gave him an odd look. "You don't have a son," he said.

"Since yesterday I do. His name is Mimi Siku. Mimi, this is my friend Richard," Michael said.

Richard held out his hand to the boy. But Mimi ran past him, off the escalator, and over to a woman in a snakeskin jacket.

"Buradu!" Mimi cried out with joy. Snakeskin! He had finally seen something that looked familiar. Mimi reached over and rubbed his hands against the rough, grainy leather. "You kill buradu?" he asked the woman. "Bite neck?" Mimi looked at the yards of snake skin. "You good hunter," he complimented her.

The woman hurried off.

"I'm sorry, he has a thing for snakes," Michael called after the frightened woman. "Take my hand, Mimi Siku," he ordered the boy.

Michael and Mimi followed Richard into the parking lot and climbed into his Chevy Blazer. As they sped off towards Manhattan, Mimi stared out of the window, mesmerized.

"This your village, Baboon?" Mimi asked.

Michael nodded. "This my village."

Mimi looked over the bridge toward the giant skyscrapers of Manhattan Island. "It big," he exclaimed.

* * *

Michael had hoped to bring Mimi to the apartment

34

and get him some decent clothes. But there wasn't time for that now. Michael had to go straight to the firm and get this coffee mess cleaned up. With luck the kid would stay locked in his office until Michael could smooth things over with Mr. Latshaw.

Michael snuck Mimi into the building through a back elevator and raced him into his office.

Mimi plopped down on the couch as Michael leafed through his magazines, in search of something that would keep Mimi busy. *Cosmo*? No. The boy wasn't ready for those models just yet. *Mac World*? Nah, what did the kid care about computers? *Car and Driver*? Bingo! What twelve-year-old wouldn't want to look at pictures of great cars?

"Look at this baby," he told Mimi, pointing to a sleek black race car. "The McLaren F1. Zero to sixty in under three seconds. I'd give anything—"

"CROMELIN!" Michael's car dreams were interrupted by a bellowing voice coming from across the hall. It was Mr. Latshaw.

Michael raised his arms, flexed his muscles, and told Mimi, "Baboon go fight chief." He turned to Madeleine. "Keep an eye on him, please?" Michael asked.

"No problem," she answered as Michael left to face Mr. Latshaw's screams. "You're a cutie," Madeleine told Mimi. "You're going to break a lot of hearts."

Before Mimi could answer her, a loud voice

disturbed their conversation. Mimi got up and peeked into the office across the hall.

"Look at this!" Mr. Latshaw shouted. "Coffee opened at eighty-eight and it's dropping like a brick!"

"If we unload it right now, we won't lose everything," Richard suggested.

"No." Michael's reply was calm and firm.

Richard looked at Michael oddly. "No?" he asked.

Michael shook his head. "No," he repeated. "If we wait it out, the market will turn around."

"What if it doesn't?" he asked.

"It will," Michael assured him. "It always does. There'll be a frost, a drought, a flood, some disaster to drive the price up. There always is. We've been here before. Remember sugar in 1991?"

"That was luck," Mr. Latshaw bellowed.

Michael shook his head. "What about cotton in '94?" he asked.

But Mr. Latshaw would not be convinced. "One of these days, the good Lord's not going to provide a natural disaster to save your miserable behinds!"

Mimi Siku had been watching the whole thing. He did not like the way that big man was shouting at Baboon. He peeked over and saw Madeleine busy on the phone. Now was his chance. The boy quietly pulled a small circular box from his bag, popped open the top, and took out Maitika—the same spider Michael had met in the jungle.

"Go!" Mimi ordered the spider. Instantly, the eight-legged creature made a beeline across the hall and into Mr. Latshaw's office.

"You seem to have forgotten, Cromelin, that you were investing the company's money!" Mr. Latshaw screamed. "When you invest the company's money and win, the company is behind you! But when you screw up like this, you're on your own. Sell the beans for what you bought them for, and if you can't, you're on the hook for the difference!"

Michael looked down at the floor and numbed himself to Latshaw's non-stop complaining. That's when he saw the tarantula.

"Shhhh . . . ," he warned. "Be quiet, Bill."

"Don't tell me to be quiet!"

Michael watched as Mimi's tarantula climbed up his boss's shoe. Michael had to get rid of the tarantula—without letting Latshaw know it was there.

"Oh my God, what's that!" Michael shouted, pointing to the ceiling.

"What's what?" Latshaw asked.

"That. There! On the ceiling! It looks like one of those alien rings! Look up there!"

Luckily, both Richard and Mr. Latshaw did as they were told. They didn't see the spider follow Michael out of Latshaw's office, across the hall, and into Michael's office.

The spider made its way towards Madeleine's

desk. Once again, Michael pointed to the ceiling. "What's that?" he cried out in false alarm.

As Madeleine looked up, Michael motioned to Mimi Siku. "Catch it!" he commanded the boy.

Mimi shook his head. "Stop shout, Baboon," the boy said proudly. "Maitika kill chief."

"Catch that thing!" Michael repeated.

Mimi was confused. But he did as he was told.

Michael watched as Mimi gently put the tarantula back in its box. Michael felt bad about yelling at the boy—after all, Mimi was only trying to help.

"Thank you, Mimi," Michael said finally. "But we no kill chief. Understand?"

Mimi nodded. Michael breathed a deep sigh. One emergency avoided. But there was still the little matter of Richard, Mr. Latshaw, and two million dollars' worth of coffee beans to attend to.

"Whatever you do in Venezuela, do not touch the *chile de fuego*," Michael excused himself, patting his stomach uncomfortably as he entered the room.

Later that evening, Richard drove Michael and Mimi to Charlotte's design studio. Michael knew Charlotte would be there waiting for him. Before he'd left, Charlotte had asked for a little surprise from South America.

Michael had a surprise for Charlotte all right.

Well, at least he didn't have to worry if it would fit!

CHAPTER TEN

Richard stopped his Blazer outside Charlotte's loft. Michael opened the car door and looked over at Richard. Give me a few minutes with Charlotte before you come up, he told him. Then he walked into the building and took the elevator up to the tenth floor.

The doors opened into a flurry of activity. Charlotte's assistants were busy at a table, maniacally cutting fabric. Richard's daughter, Karen, stood high on a platform in the corner. A seamstress was busy pinning the hem on her dress. Clothing designs hung all over the wall.

A magnificently accessorized woman emerged from the crowd and gave Michael a huge hug and a kiss. A cameraman filmed the scene.

"Michael, darling," Charlotte squealed. "Welcome home!"

Michael looked from Charlotte to the film crew that surrounded her.

"We're here, but we're not here," explained a large man.

Michael stared at him. *Huh?*

"Just act natural," Charlotte whispered in Michael's

ear. "Did you miss me, darling?" she asked in a louder, slightly affected voice.

Michael found it very difficult to "just act natural" while a camera crew taped his every sound. But for Charlotte's sake he tried. "Yes. I . . . missed . . . you . . . very . . . much," he replied, in a terribly stilted voice.

Charlotte smiled. "My pieces were such a hit that Ian—this is Ian Finch Parker—is doing a piece on me for the Fashion Channel," she explained.

"There's a Fashion Channel?" Michael asked. He regretted the words before they ever left his lips. Charlotte was a famous fashion designer and it drove her crazy that Michael didn't know anything about what she did or the people she worked with.

Luckily, because the cameras were rolling, Charlotte opted to pass over Michael's comments. "Ignore the camera," she instructed him. "Just talk to me." Charlotte shifted ever so slightly so the camera could have a better angle. "Did you get everything settled?" she asked.

"Yes. Patricia was very reasonable."

Charlotte smiled for Michael *and* the cameras. "What did I tell you?" she said cheerfully. "When you face your worst fears, they are never as bad as you thought they would be."

"Well . . ." Michael began, but Charlotte quickly interrupted him.

"There's just one little thing I want to change," she

said in a voice dripping with sugar. "The wedding date. You see, there's this great Gothic ballroom Ian has always wanted to shoot in, but it's only available at the end of *next* month."

Michael's face drooped slightly at the thought of a huge wedding in a Gothic ballroom with Ian as the photographer.

"We were going to have a video, anyway," Charlotte insisted, "and this way it will be brilliant!"

Michael shook his head. "Will you be there?" he teased her.

"Of course, silly," Charlotte grinned. "Now, what did you bring me?"

Michael forced a smile to his face. Here comes the hard part, he thought to himself. Slowly, Michael began to tell Charlotte about Mimi Siku. He watched as her face went from elated to disappointed to panic-stricken.

"Are you upset?" Michael asked her, finally.

"Everyone else I know comes back from South America with a *sombrero*. Not a child," Charlotte mumbled as she tried to absorb the news.

"I didn't plan this," Michael insisted.

"I've got a show to prepare and we're supposed to be planning our wedding."

"That's next month," he reassured her. "He'll only be here for a little while."

But Charlotte could not be calmed. She raced into her office and slammed the door behind her. As

Michael sank back into the couch, a cameraman plunged a video camera toward his face. He was waiting for Michael's response.

But before Michael could utter the four-letter word he was thinking of, the elevator doors swung open— out stepped Richard and Mimi. The camera crew stared curiously at the unusually dressed boy.

"It's a look," one man said.

"Hi Daddy! Do you like my bridesmaid's dress?" Karen called over to Richard, as she turned slowly on the platform.

Richard stared at his daughter and beamed. "You look beautiful," he told her.

"This is so much fun," she exclaimed, "I want to be a model."

Mimi Siku walked over and stared up at Karen. She was the most exotic girl he had ever seen. "Angel on table," he murmured.

Meanwhile, Charlotte was locked in her office, lighting one cigarette with the last as she paced the floor. "Look at me. I'm smoking," she moaned between drags.

"The rain forest is a very hot issue right now," Ian remarked, hoping to calm her down.

Charlotte stopped mid-pace. "You're right. Everybody's doing benefits for it. Sting. Bianca."

"It can only help you," Ian agreed.

"Where is the rain forest?" Charlotte asked, finally.

Ian shrugged. Then he opened the door and called to his assistant. "Brian, find out where the rain forest is."

Charlotte snuffed her cigarette into the ashtray, stood tall, and smoothed the creases in her skirt. "Okay," she said, "I'm better."

There was a quiet knock at Charlotte's office door. Then Michael and Mimi Siku slowly entered the room. Charlotte stared at the strange boy in the loin-cloth and headband. Mimi stared at the woman with hair the color of nothing he'd ever seen in nature.

"Mimi Siku, this is Charlotte," Michael said.

Charlotte smiled and put out her hand. "It's nice to meet you, Mimi Siku."

"This your female, Baboon?" Mimi Siku asked Michael.

Michael nodded. "Well . . . yes, she's my female."

Charlotte laughed. "As his female, I'd like to invite you . . ." Charlotte stopped mid-sentence and turned to Michael. "Why did he call you a baboon?" she asked.

"It's the hair on my chest," Michael explained.

Charlotte sighed. Of course. "And as his female," she continued, "I'd like to invite you to dinner with Baboon and Fiona Gluckman, the fashion editor of *Elle*. Is there anything special you would like to eat?" Charlotte asked.

"Monkey guts," Mimi told her.

Charlotte's face dropped.

Richard poked his head in and held up his cell phone. "It's Bob Montgomery," he whispered to Michael. This was an important call—one that could solve this whole coffee business once and for all.

"Bob," Richard said into the phone, "I'm here with Michael Cromelin. Considering our long history together, you're the first person we wanted to offer this to. We've got 5,100 tons of coffee beans, and we'd love . . ."

There was a click on the other end of the line. It was followed by a dial tone.

"We're dead," Richard said, rubbing his hands together in a panic.

"Don't panic," Michael ordered.

Richard grabbed the handkerchief from his breast pocket and wiped the beads of sweat from his face. "Do I look like I'm panicking?" he asked.

Bang! Bang! Bang! Before Richard could reply, he heard something knocking against the window. He looked up to discover Mimi Siku climbing along the outside ledge—ten stories off the ground!

"Baboon! Baboon!" the boy called proudly to his father.

Charlotte went over to the window and nearly fainted. "Michael!" she cried.

"Mimi Siku!" Michael yelled in fear.

44

But Ian seemed pleased with the boy's trick. "Marvelous! Get this!" he exclaimed to his camera crew. Then he turned to Charlotte and sang out joyously, "Life happens around you!" Clearly Mimi's trek onto the ledge had made Ian's day!

There was one other person in the room thrilled by Mimi Siku's climbing—Karen. She thought this new visitor was the greatest guy she'd ever seen. "Cool!" she called out to him.

Michael had no choice but to go out there and lure the boy back inside. Nervously, he opened a back window and gingerly climbed out onto the ledge next to Mimi Siku.

Mimi Siku smiled at his father and pointed across the New York skyline. "Statue of Liberty, Baboon," he told Michael.

But Michael wasn't thinking about tourist attractions at that moment. "Don't move, Mimi," he screamed. "Hug the wall."

"Statue not far," Mimi Siku replied. "We go now."

"I'll take you tomorrow," Michael promised, hoping to lure the boy inside. Then Michael made a big mistake. A very big mistake. He looked down. His head whirled and the breath raced from his body. "Whoa!" he cried.

"Look, people down there so far from us," Mimi said with amusement.

Michael was not as amused. "Let's keep it that

way, shall we?" he suggested. "Oh my God. I'm going to die."

Mimi Siku held out his hand. "Nothing bad happen, Baboon," he assured him. "Take my hand."

Together, they inched back toward the window. Michael was the first to crawl back into the loft. Then he grabbed Mimi Siku and dragged him back in. To the people inside it looked like Michael had saved Mimi Siku, instead of the other way around (which is just what Michael wanted them to think). Charlotte and the film crew burst into applause.

"Don't you ever, ever, ever do that to me again, young man. Do you understand me?" he scolded.

"Mimi Siku sorry," the boy replied.

Michael put his arm around Mimi Siku and gently led him to the elevator.

"Baboon scared?" Mimi Siku whispered.

"Yes, Baboon scared," Michael replied in a voice so quiet Ian's cameras could not pick it up. "Baboon not know he could be so scared."

Charlotte watched nervously as father and son got into the elevator. She was getting more and more upset. Things were going so *wrong*. This film was supposed to be about *her*—not about Michael and his window-climbing son.

Rain forest angle or no rain forest angle, the kid had better not ruin my dinner party, Charlotte thought as she pulled another cigarette from the pack.

CHAPTER ELEVEN

That night, Michael did his best to make sure Mimi Siku made a good impression at dinner. He dressed the boy in a pair of crisp khakis and a nice button-down shirt. He even tried to teach him to eat with a knife and fork.

For a while, everything went smoothly. Fiona gushed over Charlotte's designs, and Charlotte ate up the compliments. Everything went perfectly until Charlotte's cat, Coco, leaped up in Charlotte's lap.

Mimi went over and felt the cat. "Cat fat," he commented. "We eat cat."

Fiona gasped. "Excuse me?" she whispered over her champagne glass.

"Taste like chicken," Mimi assured her.

"I don't eat meat, dairy, or nightshade vegetables," Fiona explained.

Just then the doorbell rang. "This must be the food," Charlotte announced, jumping to her feet. "We are *not* going to eat the cat," she hissed to Mimi.

"Cat job, feed people," Mimi said to Michael.

"Here, cat job sleep," Michael explained. Mimi shrugged and walked off.

Charlotte paid the delivery man and took the huge bag of food from him.

"This is much too much for me," Fiona moaned. "I hope he didn't forget my tiramisu again."

Charlotte carried the food into the kitchen. Fiona and Michael followed close behind.

What they found in the kitchen infuriated Charlotte, shocked Michael, and made Fiona sick. Mimi Siku was crouched on the floor, eating the cat's food!

"This much tasty. Your female make good food, Baboon," he complimented Michael.

Fiona clasped her hand over her mouth and raced for the bathroom.

Later, after everyone had left, Michael climbed into bed and smiled sheepishly at Charlotte. "Once we got down to eating, I don't think it went that badly," he said.

"Michael, Fiona threw up," Charlotte countered. Then she sighed and changed the subject. "But never mind that. You had no right to change the rules," she insisted.

Michael looked at her curiously. "What rules?" he asked.

"We agreed that we didn't want any children,"

Charlotte told him. "We said that you'd be my child, and I'd be your child. Now I find out you've had a child all along."

Michael sat up and scowled. "Are you saying that I knew that I had a child?" he asked indignantly.

"Ian says that deep inside, every man knows when he has a child," Charlotte said.

This Ian character was really getting to Michael. "Look," he insisted, "there's no magical bond between father and son that spans continents. The only reason I found out about my child was because *you* insisted I go to the Amazon and speak up about the divorce."

"So now you're saying that you having a child is my fault?" Charlotte demanded.

Michael gave her a squeeze. "I'm kidding, Charley," he assured her. "Mimi's just visiting and I want to show him a good time. After that he'll go home and we can go back to being exactly the way we were: entirely wrapped up in ourselves."

Charlotte gave him a catlike grin. "Perfect," she purred.

The next morning, Michael and Charlotte slept in. But Mimi was up with the sun. The boy watched as a neighbor fed pigeons on her balcony. Mimi grinned. *Breakfast!* Quickly he grabbed his bow and arrow, aimed, pulled back on the bow, and . . . *thwack* . . . nailed a pigeon to the wall.

"AAAAAAAHHHHH!" the neighbor jumped up and screamed.

Her hollering woke Michael (and probably half the building). Michael ran to Mimi. "What did you do?" he demanded. Then he glanced out the window and spotted the neighbor crying in hysterics over a dead pigeon. Quickly, Michael dropped the blinds.

"You can't do that here," he explained to Mimi. "We don't kill birds for breakfast." Michael pulled down a box of cereal and poured it in a bowl. "Here, this is what we eat," he said.

Mimi stared at the square, brown nuggets. "What is?" he asked.

Michael picked up the box and read the ingredients. "It's, well, long multisyllabic words that I can't pronounce." Michael poured milk over the cereal and handed the boy a spoon. "Enjoy," he said. Then he headed into the bedroom to wake Charlotte.

Charlotte woke with a start. "What time is it?" she asked Michael.

"Seven," Michael told her. "Mimi's having breakfast now. I'll be back for lunch."

"Well, I can't watch him," Charlotte said. "*Women's Wear* is coming to the loft today."

"Do what you have to do," Michael said, as he kissed her cheek. "Mimi'll be fine."

Michael headed into the kitchen. Mimi smiled as soon as he walked in the door.

"When we go Statue of Liberty?" the boy asked joyfully.

"Tomorrow," Michael said slowly. He tried not to look as the boy's face fell. "I know I promised today, but Baboon must go work. Make big trades."

Mimi nodded. "Me go trade with Baboon," he offered.

Michael shook his head. "No. Baboon go alone. Baboon want to go with you," he explained to the disappointed boy. "But Baboon obligated to go."

Michael looked at the boy's confused face. *Obligated* was obviously not a word the Pinare used often. "That means when you have to do something even if you don't want to," he explained quickly.

"Okay, Baboon obligated," Mimi muttered.

Michael handed Mimi a white card with black lettering on it. "Here's my card," he said quickly. "You miss Baboon, you get Charlotte to show you how to call on the phone. Now promise Baboon: no shoot animals. No hunt. No eat cat."

Mimi gave his word—no shoot, no hunt, no eat cat.

Michael glanced at his watch. It was almost 7:30! He raced out the door and off to work.

Mimi smiled as the door closed. Baboon had made him promise a lot of things. But there was one thing he hadn't made him promise. And that was the one thing Mimi planned to do.

51

CHAPTER TWELVE

While Charlotte was locked in the bedroom, primping and prepping herself for the upcoming day, Mimi got ready to head out into the streets of Baboon's village. He painted his face in the best Pinare fashion and took along his bow and arrow—just in case.

Mimi walked out the door of the apartment building and squinted into the sunlight. Everywhere Mimi looked there were tall buildings, cars, bicycles, and lots and lots of people. But from the street level, he couldn't see the Statue of Liberty. There was only one thing to do. Mimi flagged down a man on a bicycle and asked directions.

"Which way Statue of Liberty?" the boy asked.

"Down in Battery Park," the man replied, pointing south. Mimi nodded and began walking in the right direction.

It took him a while, but Mimi finally made his way to Battery Park. A big grin formed on the boy's face as he looked out over the water and saw the big green statue. There she was—the woman who held fire up the sky's behind.

A huge tour boat pulled into the harbor. Mimi hopped on board and hitched a ride over to Liberty Island. As the boat sailed across the water, Mimi reached into his pouch and pulled out the same thick, sticky stuff that helped him climb mountains in the rain forest. By the time the boat docked at the island, Mimi was prepared.

Getting off the boat, Mimi felt strong and confident. Before long, he would complete the chief's task.

One by one the tourists got off the boat and took their places in the long line that led inside the Statue of Liberty. Mimi Siku looked curiously at the seemingly endless row of people and then slipped around to the front side of the statue.

Mimi started to climb up the base of the statue. Up the thick, coppery folds in her dress he ascended, over the bridge of her nose, and up to her forehead. The view from the statue's head was astounding, but Mimi didn't stop to look. He had a job to do—to get fire from the Statue of Liberty.

Finally, Mimi reached the pointed crown around the statue's head. But as he looked up at the statue's torch, he realized that there was no real fire there at all. Mimi almost cried. If he couldn't bring back the fire, how could he be a respected man of the Pinare tribe?

Down below, Mimi heard a loud commotion. The boy looked down to discover that men in blue uniforms seemed to have taken over the island.

* * *

Back at Michael's office, Richard was finally beginning to calm down. He had found a potential buyer for the coffee beans. He and Michael were going to meet with him this very morning. But just as the two men headed out the door, Madeleine stopped them.

"Mr. Cromelin," she said, "You have a call. It's the police."

For the first time in his life, Michael felt panic. Was Mimi hurt? In trouble? Michael grabbed the phone and listened anxiously to the sergeant on the other end. The sergeant explained that the police had Michael's son in custody, after bringing him down from the Statue of Liberty's head. They'd been able to contact Michael because the boy had his business card in his pouch.

"Goodbye, Sergeant, and thanks," Michael said finally, after the police officer had said his piece. "And don't worry about that sticky stuff. The first rain, and you'll never know it was there."

Michael hung up the phone and apologized to Richard. He was going to have to meet him at the buyer's office. Richard started to fidget skittishly. He didn't want to handle the meeting alone. But something in Michael's eyes told Richard that this was no time to argue.

Michael raced outside. He knocked over three

people to get into a cab. "Battery Park, and step on it!" he told the cabdriver.

The cabdriver smiled and gunned the gas. He sped through traffic, cutting off tour buses, limos, and a few bike messengers. The cabbie was a maniac. But he did as he was told. It took only a few minutes for Michael to get to Battery Park.

"I said I would take you tomorrow!" Michael told Mimi as they left the station house.

Mimi sulked. "Always tomorrow," he complained. "You too busy for Mimi Siku. Me want to see Statue of Liberty, me go."

"Mimi, I've got a life here. I can't just change everything because you showed up," Michael explained.

"Then why did you bring me here?"

Michael sighed. "Because I was obligated."

Obligated. Mimi's heart sank. Michael had told him that meant something you have to do even if you don't want to.

Mimi stood tall and glared at his father. If that's how he felt, Michael didn't have to be with him anymore! Mimi darted out into the street—right in the direction of the oncoming traffic! A city bus was coming right toward him. *Honnnnnkkkkk!* The bus driver slammed on his brakes and bashed his horn.

"MIMI!" Michael shrieked.

CHAPTER THIRTEEN

Without a thought for himself, Michael raced out into the street. "Mimi! Stop!" he cried. The boy ignored him, but turned just in time to miss colliding with the bus. Michael breathed a sigh of relief. But the relief was short-lived. A speeding delivery van turned the corner, flying in Mimi's direction. Michael reached out, grabbed Mimi's arm, and quickly pulled him to safety.

"I didn't mean it," Michael apologized, as he caught his breath on the nice, safe New York sidewalk. (At least it seemed safe in comparison to the busy New York streets!)

But Mimi knew better. Michael had meant what he said. No doubt about it. "Me want to go home," he told Michael. "You not want Mimi here."

"I do want you here," Michael insisted. "I was just angry. And I'm scared something might happen to you. This isn't Lipo Lipo, you know. My village is very dangerous."

Mimi shook his head. "Mimi Siku not scared," he declared. "Mimi Siku is a man!"

Michael wasn't going to argue with a twelve-year-old kid. He had already learned his first parental lesson: Choose your battles. Sometimes it was better just to give in. "All right, you're a man," he agreed. "But you gotta give me this: You're a short man! "

Mimi looked up at Michael. He couldn't argue with that. Mimi started to laugh. And for the first time, his father laughed with him.

"Since you're so determined," Michael grinned, putting his hand around the boy's shoulder, "I'll teach you a few things about my jungle that all men should know."

"And me teach you to use blowgun," Mimi offered. He reached into his pouch and handed the small mouthpiece to his father.

"You're on," Michael agreed. "Here's your first lesson: When you want to go somewhere in my village, stick out your hand."

Michael stepped off the curve and raised his hand high in the direction of the oncoming traffic. A big yellow taxi stopped at his feet.

Mimi's eyes opened wide. That was a great trick. Greater even than any trick the Pinare witch doctor had ever performed! "Magic," the boy whispered in awe.

Michael chuckled. "No. It's only magic if the cabdriver speaks English."

Michael told the driver to take them to an address

down near the Fulton Fish Market. There was no time to drop Mimi at home. Oh well, Michael thought as the cabdriver cut off two bicycle messengers and a little old man with a cane, the kid wants to see a champion trader at work. He may as well see me working my hardest.

The cab stopped in front of a dark, dingy fish store on one of the side streets. Richard was waiting on the sidewalk. He popped an antacid tablet in his mouth and fidgeted with his coat as he raced over to Michael.

"What took you so long?" he demanded.

Michael looked up at the sign on the store. It said CHUCK'S HOUSE OF CAVIAR. "We're meeting this guy in a deli?" Michael asked.

"He's above the deli," Richard explained.

"Oh, much better," Michael muttered sarcastically. He and Mimi followed Richard into the deli.

A white-clad clerk came out from behind the counter and led them through to a meat locker. He opened a back door and brought them to the foot of a rickety wooden staircase. Michael looked up. The staircase was dark, lit only by a single bare bulb. This place was creepy. Something here was definitely not on the up-and-up!

"When you get to the door at the top, ring the bell twice, knock once, and then ring three times," the clerk said, demonstrating with his fingers—several of which, Michael noticed, appeared to be missing.

"What happened to his fingers?" Michael whispered to Richard.

"Don't ask," Richard warned.

Security cameras followed Richard, Michael, and Mimi's every move as they made their way to the top of the stairs. When they got there, they found the door the clerk had referred to.

"Okay, ring once. Knock twice. Then ring three times," Richard said aloud.

Michael did as he was told. No one answered.

"No. No," Richard corrected himself. "It was ring three times. Knock once. Ring twice."

Michael tried that. Again, no one answered.

"No, wait. I got it," Richard insisted. "Ring once, knock twice . . ."

"OPEN THE DOOR!" a loud voice bellowed from the other side.

Michael turned the knob and pushed the door open. Slowly he, Richard, and Mimi entered the room.

The office was huge, with oversized leather furniture and a massive wooden desk. Behind the desk sat a very large man. His name was Jovovich.

Richard reached his nail-bitten fingers across the table and began to introduce himself. Jovovich stopped him in his tracks.

"Don't introduce," the man said in a thick Russian accent. "I know." He pointed to Richard. "You are Cromelin. You," he said to Michael, "are Kempster."

Jovovich looked curiously at Mimi. "And you are love child of him," he finished, pointing to Richard.

Michael shook his head. "No. I am Michael Cromelin, he's Richard Kempster, and this is *my* son, Mimi Siku," he explained.

Jovovich's round Russian face grew beet red. He looked as though he were about to explode. The big man slammed his hand against the desk. The floor shook from the force.

"Mistake. I make mistake," he bellowed. Then his face softened. "Last time," he insisted as he motioned to two overstuffed chairs. "Come, we talk beans."

Richard and Michael took their seats. Mimi rested on the arm of his father's chair and eyed the big dough-like man with skepticism.

"Coffee on market now eighty-three cents, one pound," Jovovich said. "I pay you eighty-five cents, one pound."

Richard almost leaped out of his seat. "We accept!" he declared.

Mimi scrunched his eyes up. Something here didn't make sense. "Eighty-five cents more than eighty-three cents, Baboon?" he asked Michael.

Michael nodded. Mimi stood, looked the big Russian straight in the eye, and asked, "Why you take trade?"

Jovovich got a wild look in his eye. "Jovovich not explain his business to wild child!" he declared.

Michael is the center of attention as he tries desperately to communicate with the outside world.

After recovering from the shock of discovering he has a son, Michael decides to make the best of it.

Michael and Mimi Siku—father and son—bond.

Not yet skilled at village life, Michael tries to escape a large tarantula, but ends up taking a dip.

Mimi sleeps peacefully with his pet tarantula, Maitika.

Dressing like the natives, Michael takes his place next to Patricia at Mimi Siku's tribal ceremony, which marks Mimi's passage into adulthood.

Like father, like son—Mimi paddles alongside a trader's boat and barters skillfully, exchanging a pretty stone for a pot.

It's not Armani, but Mimi's new clothes are certainly an improvement.

The pigeon on the neighbor's landing becomes a meal as Mimi Siku hunts for his breakfast.

Mimi Siku doesn't understand why his father is so frightened.

When Mimi darts through a busy intersection, Michael races after him just in the nick of time.

No, it's not the newest hair weave!

Michael tries to explain to Mimi Siku how things are done in *his* jungle.

Mimi Siku stops to dance while he is serenaded by a street performer.

Mimi Siku decides to climb the *outside* of the Statue of Liberty in an attempt to bring its fire back to his village.

Yearning for his village, Mimi paints Karen's face Lipo Lipo style as they sit around the campfire in her backyard.

Suddenly he looked across the room. A cockroach was climbing slowly up the wall. "Bug!" the big man shouted nervously.

Instantly, a tall, sinister-looking man smashed the cockroach against the wall. It dropped to the floor, dead.

"I hate bug," Jovovich explained simply.

"So, do we have a deal?" Richard butted in, before Mimi could cause any more trouble.

Jovovich hesitated. It was obvious there was something more he desired before the trade could go through. "I want guarantee that price not go below seventy," he said calmly.

"You got it," Richard assured him.

"Wait a minute!" Michael warned Richard. "No. Mr. Jovovich—this is speculation."

"He knows speculation," Richard spat out through clenched teeth. "When can we expect payment?" he asked Jovovich sweetly.

Jovovich snapped his fingers. Instantly one of his comrades entered the room with a large black suitcase. Jovovich thumped the case on his desk and with two quick snaps popped it open. Richard gasped. He had never seen so much cash in one place!

"Take. Yours." Jovovich said happily.

Richard reached for the case. Michael grabbed his arm. "Excuse us, Mr. Jovovich," Michael apologized. "I'd like to speak to my associates in private." He dragged Richard and Mimi into the stairwell.

"Are you out of your mind?!" Michael hissed when Jovovich was out of earshot. "We are not laundering money for the Russian Mafia. Besides, you know as well as I do that the price could drop out of sight!"

"And then where would we be?" Richard insisted.

"In a much better place than if we sell it to this goon and it drops below seventy. That happens, you and I will be sleeping with the sturgeon."

Richard shook his head. "That's not going to happen," he assured Michael.

Michael nodded. "You're right. Because we're not making any deals!" Michael turned to Mimi. "What do you think?" he asked the boy.

Mimi frowned. "Him big buradu," the boy said.

"Snake," Michael translated to Richard. "There you have it. Tell him no deal."

Richard watched as Mimi and Michael went down the stairs. Then he turned and went back to Jovovich's office.

A short while later, Richard was on his way back to the firm. He didn't know if Michael had returned to the office yet—but he hoped he hadn't. Richard couldn't face Michael right now.

As Richard looked at the black suitcase in his hand, he knew instinctively that Michael was *not* going to be happy about what he had just done.

CHAPTER FOURTEEN

For the moment, a blissfully ignorant Michael was having a blast! He'd just finished buying his kid some great clothes at a local teen shop, and was now busy watching Mimi wolf down his very first hot dog with the works.

Mimi looked at the crowd on the street—a turbaned East Indian man walked by next to a Hasidic Jew in a long black coat and a tall hat. Two African-American boys scooted by on Rollerblades. They were followed by a messenger with a green Mohawk riding a motor scooter.

"Many different tribes in your village, Baboon," the boy remarked.

"Yeah, I guess there are," Michael agreed.

Somewhere in the distance a street band was playing. Mimi ran ahead toward the music. Michael followed close behind. The rhythm really got into Mimi's soul. The boy stepped out of the crowd and began to dance. At first Michael was a little embarrassed. But the kid was good. Really good. And the crowd loved him. Michael went from being embarrassed to beaming with pride.

Then he became embarrassed again when Mimi reached into the crowd, took his hand, and pulled him forward.

"Come Baboon, we dance," Mimi urged.

"No." Michael said firmly. "Baboon does not dance in the street."

"I show you," Mimi said. "Do like this."

At first, Michael could barely move. But after a while, he realized his son was right—dancing was fun. It didn't take long before father and son were really *dancing in the streets*.

Late in the afternoon, Michael smiled contentedly as Mimi slept in the cab. What a day, he thought to himself. He, Michael Cromelin, had played hooky from work, eaten a street hot dog, and danced—in front of strangers! And he'd loved every minute of it. Michael couldn't wait to get home and tell Charlotte!

As the cab stopped, Michael gently nudged Mimi awake. Then the two stopped at a deli on the corner and picked up a bouquet of flowers for Charlotte. Finally, Michael and Mimi went upstairs. As they rode in the elevator, Michael fixed Mimi's collar and smiled. Michael just knew Charlotte would love the way the kid looked.

But when Michael walked in, Charlotte was no

place to be found. He looked in the living room and in the kitchen. "Charlotte, are you home?" he called out, finally.

"Michael! I'm in here!" Charlotte cried. Her muffled voice seemed to be coming from the bedroom.

Michael grinned and handed Mimi the bouquet. "You give her the flowers," he said as he opened the door to the bedroom.

Charlotte heard Michael's footsteps through the bathroom door. "Thank goodness you're here," she shrieked. "I've been in here all day. I'm being held prisoner by a giant spider."

Michael looked down. Sure enough, Maitika, Mimi's pet tarantula, had escaped from its box. And right now the eight-legged menace was trying to make its way into the bathroom!

"Get that thing in its box, now!" Michael hissed the order to Mimi Siku. At the sound of Michael's voice, the spider turned and headed for him.

"Do something, Michael!" Charlotte yelped.

"I'm doing something," Michael replied. He stomped hard on the carpet. Then he banged on some furniture. He wanted to make Charlotte think he was a big hero.

In reality, Mimi Siku just picked up the spider and put it back in its round box. Then Mimi left and went into the kitchen with his pet. Michael thrashed and yelled some more and finally opened the bathroom door.

"All clear," he said bravely.

"Are you sure?" Charlotte asked him.

Michael nodded. Then he looked innocently into her eyes and asked, "Where did that thing come from?"

Charlotte glared at him. She wasn't falling for that act. "It came from little *Dances with Wolves* out there," she shouted. "Where did you think it came from?"

Michael reached over to comfort her, but Charlotte would have none of it. So Michael went into the kitchen to find Mimi Siku and to get rid of that spider!

"Maitika scare Charlotte?" the boy asked.

Michael nodded. "Here's your next lesson on living in my village, buddy boy," he said sternly. "From now on, spiders live outside." Michael picked up the spider's box and threw the pet right through the open window. Then he turned to go back to Charlotte.

Mimi ran to the window, but it was too late. He watched in agony as the spider fell to the courtyard below.

"Maitika," Mimi cried out. Then he raced downstairs to the courtyard. Maybe, just maybe, the poor spider had survived the fall.

"To him, it's like a pet," Michael tried to explain to Charlotte as she sat crying in the bedroom.

"A dog is a pet, Michael," Charlotte huffed. "A cat is a pet. Although for your son, a cat is a dietary supplement as well!"

66

"I got rid of the thing," Michael promised.

"This has totally interrupted my creative flow," Charlotte complained, as she scrambled to dress.

"You're blowing this way out of proportion, Charley," Michael insisted. He ran off to answer the ringing doorbell in the foyer.

"Oh! So when it's my career, it's way out of proportion," Charlotte called after him as he left. "But when it's your career . . ."

Michael opened the door. Surprise! It was Ian and his film crew. Just what Michael needed.

"Ian. Great, I've really missed you," Michael deadpanned.

Ian could hear Charlotte still screaming from the bedroom.

"Is she okay?" he asked Michael anxiously. "If something dramatic has happened, it should be on film."

Charlotte rounded the corner and shot Michael an angry glare. "I have a shoot tomorrow," she explained to Ian, "but I was unable to prepare for it because I was trapped in the bathroom all day by his son's spider." Charlotte pointed accusingly at Michael.

"So the appearance of little Mowgli is straining your relationship?" Ian asked her sweetly, and a bit hopefully. A little tension was always good for a film. Charlotte nodded demurely.

That was it. Michael had had enough. Who was

this piece of human furniture to call his kid Mowgli?

"You're furniture, Ian," Michael growled. "Furniture does not talk."

Charlotte put on her coat. "Furniture might not talk, Michael, but it understands. Better than you do," she added as she left the apartment, film crew in tow.

That night, Michael took his son for a walk along the East River. He felt kind of bad about throwing the spider out the window.

"I'm sorry about the spider," Michael said quietly.

"Is all right," Mimi assured him. The boy smiled to himself and quietly patted the small box he kept in his sack. "Charlotte not like me."

Michael shook his head. Deep in his heart he knew it wasn't Mimi whom Charlotte disliked. "It's not you," Michael told him. "It's me. She's afraid of change."

"And spiders," Mimi joked. Michael laughed with him. Then suddenly the laughing stopped. "Why Paliku leave you, Baboon?" he asked.

Michael sighed. For a long time he hadn't known the answer to that one. But now, for the first time in thirteen years, he knew. "I guess I took her for granted," he said slowly.

CHAPTER FIFTEEN

The next morning, Michael and Mimi were up with the sun. Michael had a big day ahead of him. A tough day. A three-cups-of-coffee day. Today was the day Michael had to make things up to Charlotte.

But Michael had a great plan. He'd arranged for Richard and his family to watch Mimi for the day. He and Charlotte were going to spend the day spending money all around New York.

Mimi was dressed for the occasion—he'd even put on a tie! It was suddenly important to him that Michael's friends like him. Besides, Michael had told him that Karen, the beautiful angel he had seen the other day, lived in Richard's house, too.

Mimi looked out the window as Michael drove him to Richard's Westchester home. He liked watching the city skyscrapers give way to trees and green lawns. Finally, they pulled into Richard's driveway. Michael straightened Mimi's tie and rang the doorbell. Richard's wife, Jan, opened the door and escorted them to the family room. Karen and her little brother, Andrew, were already in there, arguing over who was in charge of the remote control.

"Jan, this is Mimi Siku," Michael said.

"Isn't he adorable," Jan replied as though Mimi weren't even in the room.

Karen blushed. How could her mother be so embarrassing? Then she gave Mimi a big smile. Mimi smiled back.

"Charlotte and I really appreciate your taking Mimi for the night," Michael told Jan, breaking the tension for an instant. "I put his stuff in his knapsack. He likes to sleep in his hammock." Michael looked around the room for an instant. "Where's Richard?" he asked suddenly.

"He left early for the office," Jan replied.

Michael shrugged. Then he said his goodbyes to Mimi, thanked Jan again, and headed back to the city. It was time for him to meet Charlotte for brunch.

As expected, Charlotte had chosen one of the most extravagant New York restaurants for brunch. It was one of those places where New Yorkers went to see and be seen. Usually, Michael hated those places. But today belonged to Charlotte, and she loved them.

Charlotte had been working all night, and she was very excited. Before Michael could even sit down at the table, she held up two sketches and shoved them in his face. "Which one do you like better for the flower girl?" she asked.

"That one."

Charlotte frowned. "Michael, that's the menu."

Suddenly, Michael's cell phone rang from within his jacket pocket. *Phew!* Talk about being saved by the bell! "Excuse me," he apologized to Charlotte.

"Michael, it's Richard," the voice on the other end of the phone said.

"Not now, Richard," Michael barked. "Charlotte and I are just about to . . ."

"Just look over your shoulder," Richard interrupted.

Michael turned toward the kitchen. Richard was standing there, talking on his phone, gesturing to Michael. Obviously this was a real emergency.

"Excuse me for a minute, darling," Michael apologized to Charlotte as he stood and raced toward the kitchen.

"What are you doing here!" Michael asked angrily, as a busboy inched past him and into the kitchen.

Richard popped a few more antacid tablets into his mouth and fidgeted with his jacket. "I made the deal," he said nervously.

"What deal?"

Richard took a deep breath. Michael was not going to like this—not one bit! "With Jovovich. After you left."

Michael's eyes bulged. "Are you out of your mind? You couldn't have. How did you get the contracts out of the vault without my signature?"

Richard looked sheepishly at the ground. Michael stared at him in horror.

"You forged my signature!" Michael shouted.

"I didn't forge it," Richard mumbled. "I just signed for you. I was scared we'd lose everything."

Michael sighed. "Where's the money?"

Richard held up the same black case Michael had seen in Jovovich's office. Michael could not believe his eyes. Had Richard completely lost his mind? "You're walking around New York City with a million dollars in cash?!" he asked, trying very hard not to draw attention to himself. And that wasn't easy, considering the number of waiters and busboys trying to make their way past him to get in and out of the kitchen.

"That's not the worst part," Richard told Michael. "Coffee fell below seventy this morning."

Michael felt like decking Richard. But he didn't want to risk hurting his fingers—not while he still *had* fingers. "Come on," he urged Richard. "We'll go to Jovovich. We'll say we made a big mistake and buy back the contracts from him."

Quickly, Michael dragged Richard over to his table. He put on his coat, kissed Charlotte on the forehead, and said, "I'm sorry, sweetheart. Only the most urgent problem could pull me away from you right now."

"Is everything all right?" Charlotte asked.

"Fine." Michael reassured her.

"It's just that we're gonna die," Richard explained.

CHAPTER SIXTEEN

Michael barely had time to park his car at the Fulton Fish Market lot before Richard was out the door. "If we buy those contracts back, we could lose everything," Richard whined nervously.

"We're speculators, Richard," Michael responded. "We speculate. We'll survive."

"Easy for you to say—I've got kids to support!"

Michael could feel his blood pressure rise. Had Richard forgotten about Mimi Siku? "So do I!" Michael declared.

"Yeah," Richard conceded. "But mine want Reeboks and Nintendo. Not blowguns and Kal-Kan!"

Michael couldn't argue with that. He walked into the deli and headed for the stairs. Now if he could only remember: was it three knocks and two rings, or knock once and ring twice?

As it turned out, it didn't matter. One of Jovovich's goons opened the door before they could knock. Michael and Richard practically fell into the room.

Jovovich was seated at his desk, sticking his arm all the way to the elbow into a raw sturgeon. "Beluga," he explained. "Best caviar in the world. Taste?"

Michael and Richard shook their heads nervously. "No, thank you," they said at once.

"TASTE!" Jovovich ordered. Michael and Richard jumped up to sample the salty fish eggs.

"Mmmmm. Excellent. Wonderful," Michael said.

"Very fishy. Eggy. Fishy eggy," Richard offered.

Jovovich had had enough with the formalities. It was time to get down to business. "Coffee now down to sixty-one, no?" he asked.

"We're as shocked as you," Michael assured him.

"Much lower than seventy," Jovovich said slowly, as he cracked his knuckles.

"Much lower," Michael agreed. "That's why we came down here. We made a mistake selling you the coffee futures, and we want to buy them back."

Jovovich stared curiously at Michael. This didn't make any sense. What did this Cromelin have up his sleeve?

"You lose money," Jovovich said slowly.

"That's the market. Lose the money, keep the fingers," Michael laughed nervously. He dug his hands deep into his pockets—just to be safe.

Jovovich tapped his fingers against the side of the big, slimy sturgeon. "I don't know," he said slowly.

"What don't you know?" Richard said, his voice anxiously leaping three octaves. "You're cleaning up here."

"You are shrewd men," Jovovich countered.

"Oh no, we're not," Michael said, glaring at Richard. "Shrewdness is not in the picture!"

Something in Michael's tone seemed to have assured Jovovich. And before they knew it, Michael and Richard had traded the suitcase of money for a small folder of coffee future certificates.

Michael didn't say a word to Richard all the way down the stairs. Finally, when the two reached Michael's car, Richard broke the silence.

"You're still angry at me, aren't you?" Richard asked.

Michael glared at him. Angry? Why should he be angry? First Richard didn't sell the futures like he'd asked. Then he sold them to the Russian Mafia—against Michael's will. Now Michael was out about a million dollars. What did he have to be angry about?

"I don't want to talk about it now, Richard," Michael said through clenched teeth. He got in his car and sped off.

"Don't worry about me," Richard called after the speeding car. "I'll take the train."

As Richard walked to the train station, he thought about all that had happened. Michael was right. They were out a few bucks, but at least they had their health. And health was a pretty important thing to have—especially if it's all you have. It was good to have this burden off his shoulders. Now he could go home trouble free.

At least that's what Richard *thought* . . .

CHAPTER SEVENTEEN

Richard didn't know it, but he had plenty of troubles waiting for him at home, too. It seemed Mimi Siku was having a bit of a problem adjusting to suburban life.

Richard opened the front door of his house and went directly into his den. He sat down and stared at his tropical fish tank. Those fish were supposed to relax him. He'd read it in a book. Richard stared at the tank, waiting for one of the beautiful, colorful fish to swim by. He waited. And waited. And waited some more. Then it hit him—the fish were gone!

"JAN!" he shouted. "Where are my fish?"

Jan came into the room, a small frown on her face. She knew Richard wasn't going to like this one. Mimi had fished them out of the tank and cooked them all—over a bonfire he'd built in the backyard, she explained.

At first Richard didn't say anything. Then he ordered all three children into the den.

"Did you think I wouldn't notice?" Richard sputtered at Mimi. "Those fish cost me thousands of dollars."

"Mimi didn't know what he was doing," Karen defended him.

"It's a multicultural thing," Jan added.

"They tasted really good," Richard's son, Andrew, assured his dad.

Richard sat down and put his head in his hands. "Ten thousand dollars' worth of sushi!" he cried out.

"I very sorry," Mimi said softly.

Richard looked at the boy. Suddenly all Richard wanted was for this day to end. "Everyone go to bed," he said. "It's late."

Karen and Andrew went up the stairs to their rooms. Mimi went outside and strung his hammock between two trees that grew just below Karen's window.

But Karen couldn't sleep. She could only think about Mimi. She got up and peered out her window, hoping to catch a glimpse of him sleeping. But much to her surprise, Mimi wasn't there. Then, out of the corner of her eye, Karen spotted him walking in the direction of the river. Quickly she jumped out of bed, threw on her robe, and snuck out of the house.

Karen caught up with Mimi at the river. He was standing thigh-high in the water, fishing. But Mimi wasn't using a pole, he was using his hands.

Eventually, Mimi looked up and saw Karen standing there. He smiled and motioned for her to come in. Karen hesitated—but only for a second. She threw off her robe and waded in next to Mimi. Karen watched as the boy reached into the water, cupped his hands, and pulled up a small gray fish. Then he expertly flipped the fish into a water-filled container on the riverbank.

"You want try?" Mimi asked.

"Sure," Karen replied.

Mimi wrapped his arms around Karen and showed her how to hold her hands still and wait for the fish to come to her. It took a while, but then Karen felt something wet and wiggly brush against her palms. A fish! Karen proudly scooped the fish up and walked it over to the container.

"Enough fish," Mimi said. Karen shook her head. She wasn't about to stop now. This was fun.

"One more!" she insisted.

The night was unusually cool for June. Mimi could see Karen shivering in the darkness. He gathered some dry driftwood and expertly built a small fire on the riverbank. The two twelve-year-olds huddled close for warmth. Once they were both warm and dry, Mimi reached into his waist sack and pulled out some face paints. Quietly, he painted a traditional Pinare pattern on Karen's face.

"You Pinare now," he told her. "Choose a name."

"You choose for me," Karen suggested.

Mimi knew just the name. "*Ukume*," he said in an official voice. "Means 'sound of rain on river water.'"

"It's pretty," Karen mused.

Mimi agreed. A pretty name for a beautiful angel. Slowly, he leaned over and kissed Karen gently on the lips.

Together they walked back to the house.

The next morning, Richard went outside to get the paper. As he bent to pick it up, his eyes nearly flew out of his head. He could not believe what he was seeing! Mimi and Karen were both fast asleep in the hammock. Richard raced over to the hammock and started screaming.

"You are going away to camp! Now!" he yelled at Karen.

"But we didn't do anything," Karen shouted back. She and Mimi quickly followed her father into the house.

"Not understand problem," Mimi said quietly.

Richard's eyes bugged. "I'll tell you the problem," he snarled. "You started a wildfire in my yard, ate my yellow dwarf cichlidae fish, and now you're putting the moves on my daughter!"

"That's not true!" Karen screamed. "I was putting the moves on him!"

Just then the phone rang. Richard listened for a minute to the man on the other end of the line. Then his face went white, his knees went weak, and the receiver dropped from his hands.

Michael and Richard were in BIG trouble!

CHAPTER EIGHTEEN

Richard may have been having an anxiety attack, but Michael was happily oblivious to his problems. Michael and Charlotte had spent a wonderful evening at home with a bottle of fine champagne. It was perfect. No business. No Mimi. Everything had gone wonderfully. Well, almost everything.

There *was* the cat incident.

When Michael had gone into the kitchen to pop open the champagne, he'd noticed Mimi's blowgun sitting on the counter. Just for fun, Michael had put the weapon to his lips and aimed for the trash can. Unfortunately, Michael's aim wasn't very good. The dart hit the champagne bottle, ricocheted off the toaster, and hit Coco in the stomach. Coco had been in a dead sleep ever since.

But here it was early morning and Charlotte hadn't noticed that her cat wasn't moving. Meanwhile, Michael stood on a stepping stool, calmly eating breakfast while Charlotte fitted him for his wedding suit.

Rrring. Darn. Michael frowned and stepped off the stool.

"Michael, don't you dare answer that," Charlotte ordered.

"It might be important," Michael explained as he picked up the receiver.

Before he could even say hello, the crazy man on the other end of the line began to rant and rave hysterically.

"Richard?" Michael asked. "Whoa. Whoa. Slow down."

Michael listened carefully as Richard popped three more antacid tablets and tried to speak: the price of coffee had soared. Jovovich thought Michael and Richard had tricked him. And he was one mad Russian!

"I'm on my way!" Michael said as he hung up the phone.

He turned to Charlotte. Her face was burning with anger. "I'm sorry," he said as he raced out the door.

Michael raced to Richard's house. He got there in record time, but not before Richard had gone completely off the wall. The man had already packed his minivan and was ready to take his family somewhere—anywhere. Maybe even find them a new identity in some protection program. There was only one problem. Karen and Mimi were locked in Karen's room. And Karen had decided she wasn't going anywhere with her father.

Michael found Richard pounding on Karen's door. "No sign of Jovovich?" he asked, interrupting Richard's banging.

"Not yet," Richard answered between mouthfuls of antacid tablets.

"Okay," Michael said, relieved. "Calm down. Where's Mimi?"

"Probably in some diner, picking up the waitress," Richard muttered maliciously.

"What are you talking about?" Michael asked.

"Your son spent the night in his hammock with my daughter!" Richard explained.

Michael frowned. "Was there a soup pot involved?"

Richard shook his head.

Michael shrugged. "Then there's no reason to be upset," he said with relief.

Richard stared at him. "Other than the fact that he ate my prizewinning fish, and the Russian Mafia is due here any minute, I guess not." Richard banged loudly on Karen's door. "Karen, open this door. DO YOU HEAR ME?!" he yelled.

"Stop screaming," Michael urged. "You're only making it worse."

That was all Richard needed to hear. He went ballistic! "Oh, listen to you. You've been a parent for three days and you're giving me lessons? I'm a parent. I've spent every day of the last twelve years worrying about my kids. But of course none of this matters to you because your kid is going home in two days."

Michael's face drooped. Two days. Just two days. He couldn't let his son spend their last two days together holed up in that room.

"All right, Richard, you win," Michael said. "Let's get the kids out of there." Michael walked back to the edge of the hall. He took a short run and threw himself at the door, trying to break it down. He would have done it, too, if Mimi hadn't picked that exact moment to open the door. With nothing to break his stride, Michael ran straight onto the balcony, hit the railing, and did a full gainer onto a picnic table in the yard below.

Mimi ran to the balcony. "Baboon!" he cried out in shock.

"Awesome fall, Mr. C," Andrew cheered.

"Thank you, Andrew," Michael groaned.

"I'll get the kids in the car," Richard told Michael.

But Mimi wasn't going anywhere without his father. He scrambled down the side of the house, and helped Michael to his feet. "We've got to get out of here." The family ran quickly down the stairs to the front door.

"I hate you," Karen declared to Richard.

Richard shrugged. "Good. Hate me in the car," he replied. Richard threw open the front door and came face-to-face with his biggest nightmare!

CHAPTER NINETEEN

"GIVE ME THE COFFEE CERTIFICATES!"

Jovovich and two of his big, ugly goons pushed their way past Richard into the house. The big Russian was angry. Really angry.

"You don't think I would keep certificates like that in my house do you?" Richard said sheepishly.

"Don't make me lose my temper!" Jovovich warned.

"Dad keeps everything in the bookcase. Behind the copy of *The Prophet*," Andrew volunteered.

Jovovich moved over to the bookcase and rifled through the books until he came to *The Prophet*. He yanked the certificates out from behind the book and turned angrily to Richard.

"Now I make you remember never to do this to Jovovich again," the big man said. He pulled out a sharp knife and motioned to one of his comrades. The huge goon grabbed Richard and threw him into an easy chair.

Michael and Mimi had been watching the whole thing through the side window. Now Michael had seen enough. "We've got to help them," he told Mimi.

"I have an idea," Mimi assured him. Michael watched nervously as the boy reached into his pouch, pulled out a sticky substance, and rubbed it all over his hands. Then, as quietly as he could, Mimi scaled the house until he reached a second-floor window.

As soon as Mimi was out of sight, Michael looked back through the window. Richard's hands were tied with thick ropes to the arms of his chair.

"You tried to cheat me!" Jovovich cried out. "Now you must pay! I give you choice. Which finger you lose?"

"I'm really fond of them all." Richard squirmed in his chair. "For different reasons, of course."

Boy, was Richard in a jam. But Michael wasn't worried about him any more. That's because out of the corner of his eye, Michael saw Mimi's spider, Maitika, cross the room and crawl up Jovovich's pant leg. Michael wasn't sure how Maitika had survived being thrown ten stories into a courtyard. But he sure was glad he did.

"I love that spider," Michael said to himself.

Jovovich raised his knife high above Richard's right thumb. "This finger make you remember: never—NEVER—make fool of Jovovich again!"

Richard winced. But before Jovovich could bring down the knife, Maitika crawled down the mad Russian's shirtsleeve and onto his hand. Instantly, the big bully was reduced to a blubbering coward!

"AAAAHHHHH!" Jovovich cried out. "Spider! I hate spider!"

Jovovich dropped the knife and flung Maitika from his hand. But the more the big man screamed, the more Maitika chased after him.

Finally, Jovovich found himself cowering in a corner, trapped by a three-inch spider.

That's when Michael made his move. He burst through the window with a loud yelp. Mimi slid down the stairs, leaped onto a hanging lamp, and swung over the Russian's head to Karen. Together, Mimi and Karen untied Richard from his chair.

Instantly, Jovovich's ugly comrades rushed at Mimi. Now it was up to Michael to come to the rescue. Michael reached into his pocket and pulled out the blowgun Mimi had given him. He took a deep breath and blew. The dart sailed straight for one of the big goon's heads . . . and kept on sailing, right past him and into Andrew's arm. The boy fell to the floor in a heap. *Oops!*

Luckily, Mimi was ready to defend himself. The boy extended his thumb and placed it forcefully onto a special spot on one of the criminals' necks. Instantly, the man collapsed.

That made Jovovich's second goon really mad. He lunged for Mimi. Karen picked up a vase and tried to hit the big man over the head. Unfortunately, Richard chose that moment to try to race to Mimi's rescue. *Crash!* The vase landed smack on Richard's head.

"Oh Daddy!" Karen cried out as her father slipped to the ground.

That did it. Jovovich's bodyguard was ready to tear the place apart. But Michael was ready for him. He raised his thumb and placed it on the man's neck— just as Mimi had done. Then he waited for the man to fall to the floor in a lifeless heap.

What a surprise . . . nothing happened. Except that the goon now turned his attention to Michael. He grabbed Michael's arm and twisted it—hard!

Mimi leaped across the room. "When thumb not work," Mimi explained, "Pinare do this!" The boy raised his knee and slammed the guy right between his legs.

"AAAAAHHHHHH!" Jovovich's henchman screamed out in pain. His face went white and he toppled onto the floor, out cold!

Jovovich did not care about his men at all. All he cared about was getting away from that spider. "Please," he begged Mimi, "take spider."

Michael grinned. Now it was his turn to make a deal. If Jovovich returned the coffee shares, and drove away, promising never, ever to bother them again, Mimi would put Maitika away.

It was an offer Jovovich couldn't refuse.

CHAPTER TWENTY

When it was all over, Michael and Richard shook hands. They were friends again. But Michael still had some unfinished business to take care of.

"Come on," he told Mimi. "There's somewhere we should go." Together, father and son drove off toward Liberty Island.

This time Mimi took the stairs to the top of the Statue of Liberty, just like everybody else. And this time he took the time to admire the view.

Michael took the time to see the view, too. And he suddenly realized that for all the years he had lived in New York, Michael had never been to the top of the Statue of Liberty.

Later, as he and Mimi shared a bag of doughnuts, Michael noticed that his son had become quiet.

"I fail, Baboon," the boy said finally. "I not get fire from the statue. Fire not real. Me miss Paliku. "Me want to go home."

Michael wrapped his arm around Mimi. He would be sorry to see Mimi go. But at least there was something Michael could arrange for his son.

* * *

The next day, at the airport, Michael handed Mimi back his blowgun. "You'll probably need this," he said.

Mimi shook his head. "You keep," he told Michael. "When you kill fly, you real Pinare. Secret: not aim where fly is. Aim where fly is going to be."

"I'll practice so I can come hunt with you," Michael promised the boy.

"You never come to Lipo Lipo," Mimi said matter-of-factly.

Just then Mimi's flight was announced over the loudspeaker. Michael handed Mimi a small gift-wrapped box. "This is for you," he said. "Open it on the plane." Then Michael pulled a small green statue from his pocket. It was a cigarette lighter shaped like the Statue of Liberty. Michael flicked the switch in the statue's back. Real fire shot up from her torch.

Mimi smiled broadly. Michael had kept his wakatepe. Now Mimi could be a respected adult in his tribe. Michael raised his hand to touch his son's cheek gently. But Mimi moved away. "Me not cry," Mimi said. "Me a man."

And as Michael watched his son walk alone toward the plane he whispered, "Yes. You are."

CONCLUSION

After Mimi left, Michael tried to get his life together. He planned a romantic getaway with Charlotte—but Ian messed it all up. Michael's romantic plans interfered with a very important chiropractor appointment the filmmaker had, and Charlotte couldn't bear to go away without him. So the getaway was put on hold. And suddenly, Michael felt very out of place in his own home.

On the office front, Mr. Latshaw and the other traders were thrilled with the money Michael had brought in from his coffee futures deal. In fact, some of the traders on the floor were already calling him a legend. Oddly enough, that didn't seem to make Michael happy either.

Then something happened that changed Michael's whole life . . . he shot a fly with Mimi's blowgun!

Back in Lipo Lipo, Mimi was making a few changes in his life, too. He had asked his mother to help him learn to speak English as nicely as Baboon did. Patricia was glad to help.

"And then the captain rang the bell," Mimi read slowly from one of Patricia's old novels. He was interrupted by a sharp beeping sound—the cell phone Michael had given him as a gift when he boarded the plane.

Mimi jumped up to answer the call. There was only one person who knew the number. "Baboon!" Mimi shouted happily into the receiver.

"I nailed a fly," Michael announced to him.

"No. You lie."

"You don't believe me? I'll show you," Michael insisted.

Mimi's heart skipped a beat. His father was coming to Lipo Lipo! "When?" he asked excitedly. "Tomorrow?"

"How about right now?" Michael asked.

Mimi looked over at the doorway of the hut. "Baboon!" he cried out. He raced into his father's arms.

Michael lifted Mimi high off the ground, spun him around, and placed him back on the ground. Then he reached into his shirt pocket and pulled out a skewered fly.

"You Pinare now, Baboon." Mimi congratulated him. "You come live Lipo Lipo?"

"For a while," Michael agreed. "You teach me to hunt?"

Mimi smiled from ear to ear. Michael smiled back.

Then he reached into his backpack and pulled out a huge Teflon-coated saucepan.

"Maybe you could use this," Michael said with a wink.

Mimi glanced at the pot and got a faraway look in his eyes. He didn't have much interest in the girls in Lipo Lipo anymore.

"How's Karen?" he asked, quietly.

"Why don't you ask her yourself?" Michael suggested. Mimi looked over at the cell phone. Michael shook his head and pointed out the window toward the water.

Mimi couldn't believe his eyes. Karen and her family were climbing slowly out of a broken-down motorboat.

"Ukume!" Mimi welcomed her.

Karen jumped overboard and climbed on shore. "Mimi!" she cheered as she threw her arms around his neck.